The M

The Mysterious Librarian

Dominique Demers

Translated by Sander Berg

Illustrations by Tony Ross

ALMA JUNIOR

ALMA BOOKS LTD
3 Castle Yard
Richmond
Surrey TW10 6TF
United Kingdom
www.almabooks.com

The Mysterious Librarian first published in French by Éditions Québec
Amérique in 1997
This translation first published by Alma Books Ltd in 2017
© Dominique Demers, 1997

Translation © Sander Berg, 2017

Inside and cover illustrations by Tony Ross. Illustrations first published
in France by Éditions Gallimard Jeunesse
© Éditions Gallimard Jeunesse, 2004

Printed in Great Britain by CPI Group (UK) Ltd, Croydon CR0 4YY

ISBN: 978-1-84688-415-3

Contents

The Mysterious Librarian

Chapter 1

Books and Mouse Droppings

It all began one Tuesday in May, at noon on the dot. Mayor Mark Peevish had plonked his huge bottom on his chair and planted his feet on his desk. He was about to tuck into a ginormous pastrami sandwich when suddenly there appeared a strange old lady right in front of him. She was very tall and very skinny and seemed to come out of nowhere. She was wearing a massive hat and a long blue dress, which was quite elegant, although it had seen better days.

"I've come… umm… I've come for the post of…. umm… librarian," she muttered in a mousy voice.

Mark Peevish was so surprised that he nearly choked on his sandwich. He put his feet back on the carpet, and his magnificent tower of sixty-four slices of meat, dripping with mustard and fat, collapsed all over his desk.

A few minutes later, she had been hired. For the first time in its history, the town of Saint-Anatole had a librarian. The mayor couldn't quite believe it. They had been advertising for the post in a local newspaper for the last thirty years, but no one had ever shown any interest, because the library was not much bigger than a broom cupboard, and the few old books it had were covered in mouse droppings.

That beanpole of a woman must be bonkers, the mayor thought when the new librarian had left his office. What was her name again?

He picked up the contract to have a look. Having wiped off some bread crumbs, he found her signature in between some splotches of mustard: *Miss Charlotte*.

"Blinking beaver hats! She doesn't even have a surname," the mayor said to himself, a little bemused.

But then he shrugged his shoulders and began to put his sandwich back together again. Actually, he was no more interested in the library and its new librarian than he was in determining the sex of a blue-footed booby. What Mark Peevish enjoyed was bossing about his secretary, watching boxing matches on the telly and stuffing his face with pastrami sandwiches. He had never opened a book in his life.

Chapter 2

A Most Peculiar Librarian

Miss Charlotte uttered a shrill cry when she entered the teeny-weeny library. A fat, juicy spider had just brushed against the tip of her nose.

A few minutes later Miss Charlotte was busy removing spiderwebs, sweeping up mouse droppings and dusting off books. When the little room was clean at last, the new librarian, in her beautiful, neat handwriting, drew up a list of everything that was there:

- *One hundred and sixty-three complete books*
- *Two hundred and two mouse-eaten books*

- *Seven huge black, hairy spiders*
- *Two smaller ones (possibly baby spiders?)*
- *Five mice*

Chuffed with the work she had accomplished, Miss Charlotte rested a little while. That's when her eye fell on the biggest spider of the lot. It was sitting on a book and didn't move.

"Poor little darling! You look all depressed!"

The spider slowly moved its long trembling legs, whereupon Miss Charlotte concluded that it had replied: "It's true."

She felt a pang in her heart and delicately picked the spider up and put it in her hand.

"You are not as ugly as all that," she said, to cheer it up. "Don't worry, I'll find you a little corner."

A few minutes later the new librarian left a note underneath the door of the mayor's office.

Dear Mr Peevish,
We must absolutely buy some new books.
A thousand dollars will be enough to start

with. Please be so kind as to slip the money under the library door.

With sincere thanks,

Miss Charlotte

Immensely proud of what she had achieved, the librarian left the Town Hall, whistling a tune. She was a bit tired after all that hard work, but she was convinced she was really going to like her new job. And more than anything else, she couldn't wait to meet the local children.

"I'm sure they'll be there tomorrow," she said, hurrying along joyfully.

That evening, Leo, the son of the woman who owned Saint-Anatole's pet shop, wrote a letter to the girl he had been dreaming about ever since last summer. He had already written tons of letters to Marie, but they had all ended up in the waste-paper basket. This time, however, he had a perfect excuse to actually put his letter in the post.

Dear Marie,

Do you remember me? I'm Leo… the boy who removed those leeches from your back last summer at the Explorers' Camp.

One evening, when we were all sitting around the campfire, you told us a story of a very tall and very skinny old lady who was always talking to her pebble called Gertrude, which she kept under her hat. She covered for your old teacher for a few months before she disappeared. You told us she was very, very strange. And very kind too. We all had the feeling you liked her a lot.

Do you think it is possible that your old teacher could the same person as our new librarian? Late this afternoon a lady just like the one you described came into our pet shop. She said she was our new librarian. Her voice was as soft as a kitten's fur and she seemed VERY odd indeed.

Believe it or not, she wanted to buy… spider food! My mum thought she was joking, but she was dead-serious. In the end she left the shop with a massive bag of mouse food, which she transported to the library on a little cart she pulled along.

Her name is Miss Charlotte, and she really is a lot like the lady you talked about, except that she doesn't have a pebble. I know this because she took off her hat to scratch her head.

Write back soon,

Leo

Chapter 3

A Reading Session

The next day, when she had finished feeding her mice, Miss Charlotte did what she thought a good librarian ought to do. She opened a book and started to read it so she could classify it and put it on the right shelf.

When he walked past the door of the library a few minutes later, Mark Peevish heard a dreadful noise. It sounded like the loud snores of an ogre who has just eaten a whole class of children.

"You're not paid to sleep!" the mayor thundered, while Miss Charlotte opened her eyes wide.

She'd fallen asleep in the middle of reading her book!

Mark Peevish used the opportunity to tell that big birdbrain that there wouldn't be any new books for Saint-Anatole's library that year.

"I'll have you know, miss, that money doesn't grow on trees! We have two bridges to build, and three roads to tarmac and twelve pavements to repair," he grumbled, and then he left.

Miss Charlotte was flabbergasted. Bridges, roads, pavements… but what about books? They are just as necessary and useful and important.

"But… but books… books are essential!" she stammered, still reeling from the news she had received.

The poor librarian suddenly felt herself all alone and demoralized. She longed to pour her heart out to Gertrude, her precious pebble. But Gertrude was gone. Someone else was now looking after her, talking to her and stroking her little round, smooth back.

But Miss Charlotte wasn't going to let the mayor get her down. There and then she decided she would find a way to get new books, whatever it would take.

"Too bad for that blockhead of a mayor!" she said aloud.

To cheer herself up, the new librarian started picturing huge piles of beautiful books. None of those boring tomes like the one that put her to sleep, no siree!

She imagined fabulous books, books that make you laugh, cry, shiver and dance. Books that take you to the far-flung corners of the earth. Books that tickle your brain, touch your heart and lift your spirit.

The new librarian drew a sigh and took another book off the shelf.

At three in the afternoon, she put her seventy-second book in a big box that was labelled: USELESS.

"Yuck! All those books are as disgusting as old, overcooked broccoli," she said.

Before attacking her seventy-third book, which she guessed would be as deadly boring as the previous ones, Miss Charlotte took a large handful of raspberry-flavoured sweets out of one of the pockets of her dress. Only then did she open her next book. But this time something magical and enchanting happened. Something absolutely marvellous and extraordinary.

Chapter 4

Sucked up by Bluebeard

Leo couldn't stop looking at the clock. He had enough of Mrs Circumflex talking about curly C and kicking K. He was in a hurry to see the new librarian again.

"If the bell doesn't ring within thirty seconds, I will scream so loud that Mrs Circumflex will have no choice but to chuck me out of the classroom," he promised to himself.

Fortunately the bell rang almost immediately, and nine minutes later Leo pushed open the door of the library.

What he saw gave him a shock.

Miss Charlotte was lying on the floor, motionless and with an open book in her hand.

Leo thought she might be dead.

He hurried towards her, took her wrist and felt a weak pulse, a sign that the heart of the new librarian was still beating.

Leo tapped her cheeks and hands. He sprinkled cold water on her and shook her, first softly and then a bit more vigorously. But Miss Charlotte wouldn't wake up. Not sure what to do next, Leo pinched her nose, breathed

into her neck and pulled her ears. He tickled
her, scratched her and shook her some more.
But nothing happened. Miss Charlotte just lay
there, stock-still.

He should of course have warned the mayor or
his secretary. Or maybe the caretaker, a doctor,
the police, the fire brigade… But instead, Leo
picked up the book Miss Charlotte had been
reading.

Bluebeard, by Charles Perrault, it said on the
cover.

Unable to resist the temptation, Leo began to read the story out loud from the point where Miss Charlotte had got to when she passed out.

It was the bloodiest and scariest story he had ever read. Miss Charlotte had got to the bit where the seventh wife of the monstrous Bluebeard opens a door to a forbidden room in the castle and discovers that the floor is covered in puddles of blood, reflecting the bodies of several women lined up against the wall, all dead.

"Yuck!" Leo burst out.

And he continued reading.

A few seconds later Miss Charlotte let out a soft groan, opened her eyes and gave him a beaming smile.

"I *love* scary stories," she said, stretching herself like a cat.

That evening Leo wrote another letter.

Dear Marie,
You're not going to believe this.
This afternoon our new librarian was SUCKED UP by a book. She was reading a

horror story and then... it's hard to explain...
she, like, fell into the story.

I was the one who found her. She was lying flat
on the floor, as dead as a dodo, or as good as.

I was also the one who brought her back.
I didn't even mean to do it. I just continued
reading out loud the story she had been in
the middle of, and then she started to move
again.

When she woke up, she was all excited. She
wanted to write a letter to the author, Charles
Perrault, to invite him over for dinner and
ask him if he had written other stories that
were just as good.

Would you believe it?

Charles Perrault wrote Bluebeard three
hundred years ago. I know this because
my dad teaches literature at uni. Surely Mr
Perrault must be dead by now.

I would have thought a librarian should
know these things, right? Unless of course our
new librarian ISN'T A REAL LIBRARIAN.
What do you reckon?

The more I think about it, the more I am convinced that Miss Charlotte is the same person as your old teacher, the one who used to talk to her pebble. Although, as I wrote before, our new librarian doesn't have a pebble under her hat.

What do you make of all this?

Write back soon,

Leo

Chapter 5

Miss Charlotte on the Front Page

That morning, on his way to work, Mark Peevish was wondering if he had made the right choice in employing a librarian.

"Books! All they do is collect dust. The telly is so much better. I am not going to spend a *dime* on buying bundles of useless printed stuff."

The mayor of Saint-Anatole walked with a firm step, muttering into his moustache. Had he looked up and around a little, the poor man would have undoubtedly swallowed his dentures.

Miss Charlotte was walking down the pavement of Saint-Anatole's high street dressed as a sandwich-board woman. On the boards hanging on either side of her body, passers-by could read:

HELP!
THE LIBRARY
IS DYING
OF HUNGER

Miss Charlotte was holding out her hand like a beggar. Townspeople walked by in a hurry. Some of them gave her a few coins without bothering to read the sign.

At noon Miss Charlotte had collected the ridiculous sum of three dollars and twenty-seven cents. Sad and disappointed, she thought about Gertrude.

"My poor little pumpkin! If only you knew what kind of job I have ended up doing. I miss the school and the children. And I'm wondering how it will all turn out."

At that moment Georges Guilbert, a journalist with the *Daily Chronicle,* spotted Miss Charlotte and decided to interview her.

Miss Charlotte told him everything: about the spiders, the mouse droppings, the mouse-eaten books, as well as the deadly boring ones. Georges Guilbert thought the new librarian was something else, and really quite nice. He took lots of notes and photographed the sandwich-board librarian.

Miss Charlotte was curious to know what that "little thingumabob" was he held in his hands. As if she'd never seen a camera before!

"You're quite the joker, aren't you?" the journalist replied, and said goodbye.

The next day a photograph of the librarian as a sandwich-board woman-stroke-beggar appeared on the front page of the *Daily Chronicle*. The town's citizens found out that their mayor was a cheapskate who refused to buy books for the library, even though he had enough money to build bridges.

Mark Peevish discovered the article on his desk just as he was getting ready to tuck into another impressive tower of sliced bread and pastrami. For the second time that week the mayor lost it and scattered his sandwich all over the floor.

"What?! Rrraa! That old witch of a librarian! If I could, I'd wring her neck. I'd string her up by her ears. I'd fry her in my frying pan along with my rib-eye steak."

Smoke was coming out of his nostrils.

He decided to sack Miss Charlotte on the spot, but then he suddenly remembered the upcoming elections. All that bad publicity would no doubt ruin his chances of being re-elected. His opponent, that sly old Frederick Finaldi, who was gunning for the post of mayor, might even use Miss Charlotte against him.

Annoyed and disappointed, he realized he could not fire Miss Charlotte.

He stayed in his seat for a long time, boiling with rage and biting his nails one by one, spitting the trimmings onto the ground.

"Oh no, you're not going to get away with this!" he roared all of a sudden.

Mark Peevish rang Georges Guilbert. First he tore a strip off him. Then he let him know that he had always intended to give the library ten thousand dollars to spend on new books.

"I was going to announce it this morning. The cheque has already been signed," he added, to convince the journalist.

Chapter 6

Dirty Books

When they walked into the playground during break, the children of the Ampersand School spotted an old lady sitting in the little park next to their building. She was very tall and very skinny, and she was wearing a massive hat. She was sitting under a tree, reading a book.

All throughout break, she just sat there, stock-still. At lunch, she was still there, with her nose stuck in a book. But at half-past four, when the school bell rang at last, she had gone.

The next day she was back, though, beaming with joy and full of energy.

This time she had brought a cart with stacks of brand-new books. The children spied on her during morning break and lunch. She was like a statue. She never moved and always seemed to be absorbed in a book, as if she were hypnotized.

At half-past four she was still there. Martin, the biggest pain in the backside of the whole school, perhaps even the whole world – the kind of boy who drives all the teachers up the wall – decided to have a closer look at that "funny old scarecrow". Half the class, including Leo, followed him.

The children jumped around Miss Charlotte, did somersaults and clambered up the tree next to her. They shouted and screamed and laughed like crazy, rolling on the ground. They barked like seals, croaked like toads, chattered like monkeys, but to no avail. The strange old lady did not move a muscle.

Martin was about to take her hat off when Leo had an idea. He took the book out of her hands and, casually and out loud, continued reading the story.

Pirates were attacking each other with their swords. The sharp blades whistled through the air as their ship was tossed by a storm. After three sentences, Miss Charlotte batted her eyelids, sighed and said in a strange voice:

"Phew! That was a close shave."

That was when the children discovered that the strange old lady, whom Martin had called "that scarecrow", was their new librarian. She pampered her new books as if they were her babies, taking them out for walks on her little cart, because no one came to the library.

"It's my mobile library," she declared, pointing proudly at the heap of books.

Martin stepped forward and rummaged around a bit before exclaiming:

"Your books are rubbish!"

Ignoring what he had said, the other children inspected the books. There were loads of different kinds of books, some with lots of pictures, others with none at all. Some titles seemed very funny, while others looked like they were romantic or very, very scary. A few

of the children wanted to borrow a book, but they didn't dare ask, because Martin and his gang would have called them idiots.

"We only like dirty books," announced Martin all of a sudden.

And he added, just to make himself clear: "Books with bare bottoms in them!"

32

CHAPTER 6

"Dirty books?... umm... With bare bottoms in them?... Well, umm... Sure. You're absolutely right. I will bring some tomorrow," Miss Charlotte promised, as she got up to leave.

And, pulling her cart along, she left, giving the children a beaming smile.

Chapter 7

Show Us Them Bare Bottoms!

Martin was convinced that Miss Charlotte wouldn't show her face again. But the next day, at break, there she was, sitting in her usual place, reading.

The children rushed towards her and Martin cried out:

"Where are my dirty books?"

Fortunately Miss Hyphen, who was on duty, was looking after a nursery pupil who had grazed his knee. The little lad was screaming so loud you would think he was having his leg amputated.

Thanks to his hollering, the teacher on duty didn't notice what was going on.

"Quickly, show us them bare bottoms," demanded Martin, gasping with excitement.

Miss Charlotte gave him a mischievous smile and picked out a book called *The Great Love of Peter Pig*.

"What?!" Martin cried out, offended. "That's not dirty at all."

"Some people think pigs are *very* dirty," answered Miss Charlotte teasingly.

Martin didn't know what to say. Miss Charlotte was absolutely right.

"But there are no bare bottoms!" Martin protested.

"Bare bottoms? But it's full of them!" Miss Charlotte replied.

And once again, she was right. Peter Pig didn't wear any underwear. As a result, you could see his big, plump, pink bottom on virtually every page.

"But that's a children's book!" Martin grumbled, furious at not having the last word.

Still, he stayed and watched how Miss Charlotte spread out her books on the lawn.

The titles and covers really made you want to read them.

The books had titles like: *Dead Bodies in the Desert*, a horror book; *The Mystery of the Jelly Babies*, an adventure and mystery story; *All You Ever Wanted to Know about Number Two*, a very funny and informative book about all sorts of poo; and *The Practical Joker's Manual*, a book jam-packed with ideas for pranks.

Leo felt strangely excited looking at all those titles. It was as if he had suddenly become very hungry. Except that instead of feeling like biting into a big fat chocolate-glazed doughnut or a hotdog as long as his arm, he felt like devouring those books.

Just as he was reaching for *The Mystery of the Jelly Babies*, the bell rang.

"Aw shucks!" exclaimed some of the other children, who were also about to reach for a book.

At the end of the afternoon, the children found a note pinned to the bench in the little park next to the school, where the new librarian had been reading her books.

I'LL BE WAITING FOR YOU
IN THE LIBRARY
MISS CHARLOTTE

Ten minutes later, when Martin McFaggin and his gang were sneakily smoking their cigarettes, a swarm of excited children invaded the library.

Chapter 8

The Librarian Is Dead!

Miss Charlotte had moved the library to the loft of the Town Hall. She was no longer working in a broom cupboard, but in a huge reading room. She'd made it so much more fun!

To start with, the books were no longer standing in serried ranks on shelves. They were scattered all over the place. Some were piled up in towering stacks, while others were tucked away in the nooks and crannies of the vast loft.

Miss Charlotte had not arranged her books by subject or in alphabetical order, like librarians always do. She had arranged them by colour: all the red books in one place, all the green ones in another. Once more Leo found himself thinking she was probably not a properly trained librarian at all.

While he was looking for *The Mystery of the Jelly Babies* he made a strange discovery. He came across a very narrow and very long bed in a faraway corner at the back of the loft.

It looks like Miss Charlotte's bed, Leo thought. Could it be that she sleeps in the library? Does she not have a flat or a house?

Underneath the bed he found a big box in which seven big hairy spiders were sleeping, wrapped in their cobwebs. A bit farther along, he nearly tripped over a bowl of grain and caught sight of a mouse running to its hole in the wall.

"Such a strange library!" Leo said to himself.

He was about to continue his exploration when one of the children cried out:

"The librarian is dead!"

Leo felt his heart leap in his breast. He ran to Miss Charlotte, who was lying flat on the floor, utterly immobile. Some of the children were shaking her and others were pinching her nose.

"Get out of the way! She is not dead," said Leo. "She has been… err… sucked up."

"*Th*ucked up? You mean with a *th*traw?" Lily, a little girl from Year Two, asked surprised.

Leo told the other children about the extraordinary discovery he had made a few days before.

"When she reads a book that is really, really exciting, Miss Charlotte gets sucked into the story. Her body stays here, but her mind is elsewhere. To bring her back to reality, you need to continue the story she was in the middle of and read it out loud.

Leo was about to give a demonstration when the mayor burst into the library like a whirlwind.

"Where is she hiding? I will make minced meat of her!" he growled.

Mark Peevish really looked very, very… *peeved*.

"That crummy librarian!' the mayor spluttered. "The caretaker has just informed me that she secretly keeps mice and spiders. Ha! Why no crocodiles as well? I hired a librarian, not a zookeeper."

In his fury, Mark Peevish forgot to look at the floor. The children quickly covered the librarian up with books.

Just in time…

"Just look at this mess," the mayor said, pointing at the heap of books under which Miss Charlotte was lying.

Then little Lily had a brilliant idea, which saved the new librarian's job.

"Mi*th* Charlotte went to look for pla*th*tic covers for her book*th*, Mister Peedoff... err... I mean, Peevish. Good idea, no?" she said, giving him her most angelic look.

The mayor left, grumbling, and Leo got to work.

The book Miss Charlotte was holding in her hand was *Matilda*. Leo read the story out loud, and while all the children were fantasizing about having this wonderful girl as their best friend, Miss Charlotte woke up quietly.

"Oh, hello children. What a great journey that was. That Matilda is quite something!"

That evening, Leo wrote another letter to Marie, even though she had not given any sign of life.

Dear Marie,
Did you get my previous two letters?
Are you ill? In hospital? On holiday?
I really wish you were here. Our new librarian is really out of this world.
Before, I wasn't too keen on books. That's changed now. Miss Charlotte says that

opening a book is like switching on a telly in your head. And that with a book you are never alone.

She always carries a book with her in her pocket. When she is sad or bored, or when she is tired of her life, her town, her friends or her country, she opens a book.

And if you could just see our library! It's chock-a-block with great books. There is no furniture, however, because Miss Charlotte ran out of money. But we can bring along anything we like.

Talking about which, I was thinking about our old tent, the one with holes in it. I love reading in a tent by the light of a torch. If I put it up in the library, it would be like being back at summer camp. Except that you won't be there.

Write to me as soon as you can. I think about you a lot.

Leo

Chapter 9

Beauty and the Beast

Not long after the arrival of Miss Charlotte, the citizens of Saint-Anatole began to be suspicious of their new librarian. The grocer was the first to get worried. First of all, Miss Charlotte only ever bought pasta and nothing else. Then one morning she asked him:

"Do you think Matilda has profiteroles for breakfast?"

Mr Canister nearly choked on his cigar. Like all the citizens of Saint-Anatole he rarely opened a book. However, he had seen the film *Matilda* on television, so he knew she was just a character in a story. But the new librarian talked about Matilda as if she really existed.

The next day Miss Charlotte wanted the postman to tell her who receives more letters: Cinderella or the Queen? She also rang the police to make sure that Bluebeard was behind bars.

Her reputation suffered a further blow when one day the children were seen bringing all sorts of unusual objects to the library, like beach umbrellas, garden chairs, blankets, cushions, torches, candles and much more. Fortunately, the parents had no idea that their children were also secretly bringing in bags of Jelly Babies, Skittles, Maltesers and other sweets that are normally not allowed.

The situation didn't improve when the teachers of the Ampersand School discovered that their pupils were hiding novels under their exercise books and were falling asleep in their desks because they'd stayed up all night reading. To make matters worse, quite a few of them preferred to immerse themselves in books, where they could hunt for treasures, capture bandits or fight hideous monsters, rather than doing their homework.

The grown-ups got together, and one evening a delegation of townspeople paid a surprise visit to the library.

There they were confronted with quite a spectacle.

The library in the loft was crammed with children, animals, books and all sorts of other unexpected things. A dwarf rabbit darted in between the legs of a parent, and two guinea pigs scurried around the feet of another. The butcher found his son sitting underneath a beach umbrella in his swimming trunks, absorbed in a novel. All the children were reading. Miss Charlotte was walking around, pouring out large glasses of grape juice.

The parents had a powwow in a corner of the library. One of them suggested they should warn the authorities about Miss Charlotte.

"She's a cheat! A fake librarian!" he shouted.

But most of the parents were impressed by the way in which Miss Charlotte had managed to pass on her passion for reading to the children. The members of the delegation spoke for a very long time. In the end, they quietly slipped away, a bit shaken by the strangeness of the place, but thinking they probably ought to reassure the other residents.

After a few weeks, the library had become a kind of HQ for the children of Saint-Anatole.

In order to give Miss Charlotte the chance to read as well, the children had divvied up her tasks. They helped the librarian by putting new covers on books and sorting them out and stamping them. They also fed the animals, cleaned the place and prepared snacks.

All the while, Martin and his gang were hanging out near the library, visibly curious, but too proud to admit they were interested.

And, like before, Miss Charlotte allowed herself to be sucked up by her books. In the beginning the children would wake her up immediately, but Leo soon realized that Miss Charlotte was disappointed to be back in the real world.

So the children decided to rescue her only when she was in a tricky situation, for instance when she was facing a sticky monster, a bloodthirsty buccaneer or a carnivorous dinosaur.

One evening, late at night, while his parents were watching television, Leo sneaked out.

His three letters to Marie had been returned to him with the words "Not Known at this Address. Return to Sender" written on the envelope. He was sad and upset, and he felt like talking to Miss Charlotte.

When he arrived at the library, he discovered that the new librarian had been sucked into *Beauty and the Beast*. Thinking she might be scared, he thought he'd better come to her rescue.

Out loud, he read the bit where Beauty discovers the Beast's present to her: a large chest full of golden dresses, studded with diamonds. But it didn't make Miss Charlotte come round from the book. So he read the passage again, this time a little louder than before. But Miss Charlotte didn't move. Worried, Leo started a third time, putting all his feelings into it. And Miss Charlotte began to yawn.

"I'm in love," she whispered as she woke up, her heart thumping and stars shining in her eyes.

Leo had realized a while back that the new librarian mixed up books and reality. So now she'd actually fallen in love with a character.

"I'm sure that the Beast thinks you are very pretty," he said, to be nice.

Feeling flattered, Miss Charlotte blushed to the roots of her hair.

Then Leo confessed that he was in love too.

"Her name is Marie. Last summer, at the Explorers' Camp, I didn't dare to get close to her, but I watched her and heard her talk. Afterwards I wrote to her, but she has moved house. I will probably never see her again," he said, his voice trembling with emotion.

Miss Charlotte looked at him for a long time without saying a word.

"If only I had my dear pebble... Oh yes! If I had my darling Gertrude, I would lend her to you," she told Leo, who was slightly puzzled.

Then she added in a serious voice: "When you're truly in love, you always find a way."

When he got home, Leo made a list of all the possible ways he could think of to find Marie. He could ring the Explorers' Camp. Maybe they could give him her new address or telephone number, or else her best friend Léa's.

Marie had often talked about her grandmother, who lived near a lake somewhere in the Laurentians. Something-something Lake... Shucks! He couldn't remember the name. But maybe he'd recognize it if he looked on a map of Quebec?

"Miss Charlotte is right. I must do everything I can to find Marie," Leo muttered to himself before falling asleep.

Chapter 10

Chips with Camembert

"Are you going to ask us trick questions to see if we've actually read the whole book?" Céline asked, a little worried, when the new librarian announced she wanted to set up a book club.

Miss Charlotte laughed wholeheartedly.

"Trick questions? Of course not. And why would I want to force you to finish a book that you find tedious?"

Leo felt relieved. His mum always told him that you had to finish what you start. With that argument she always made him finish his plate, even if it was shrivelly peas. He didn't want to have to do the same with books.

Miss Charlotte organized a big picnic to celebrate the first meeting of the book club. She invited all the children to bring their favourite dish. She didn't want to say anything else.

That evening, Mark Peevish could no longer control himself and simply *had* to see what was going on at the library.

The poor man nearly had a fainting fit. He had to leave the place in a mad panic, because his heart nearly gave out.

CHAPTER 10

Leo had brought lasagne with three kinds
of cheese, and Melanie a pepperoni pizza.
Matthieu arrived with a pork pie, while Agathe
carried cones filled with chips and camembert
– a recipe she had made up herself. All the
children had something exciting to eat in front
of them.

In the parking lot behind the Town Hall,
Martin and his gang were effing and blinding.
They swore that books were stupid, boring,
useless, tedious and only fit for morons and

dimwits. And yet they wanted to get into the library more than anything else.

Miss Charlotte had prepared her speciality: pasta medley, a big bowl filled to the brim with elbow macaroni, spaghetti, farfalle, fusilli, linguine, penne and gnocchi with a big lump of butter and parsley.

"What are you waiting for? Dig in!" said the librarian, plunging her fork into her steaming bowl of pasta medley.

The children did not wait to be told twice. They devoured their favourite dish and tried some of their neighbours' food too. Bowls and plates were being passed around all the time.

When they had finished, Miss Charlotte asked Louis to describe what he had felt when he was savouring his spaghetti with dynamite sauce.

Louis thought for a bit and then answered:

"I love the tickly feeling spaghetti makes when it rolls around my tongue. And my dad's dynamite sauce is like fireworks going off in your mouth. It's… exciting. And absolutely delicious."

The other children listened to him, their mouths watering. Even though their bellies were full, they all wanted to taste his fireworks spaghetti.

"Wonderful!" said Miss Charlotte, congratulating him. Now tell us, in exactly the same way, about the best book you have ever read.

That evening Leo left the library with plenty of books in his head. He had really enjoyed talking about *Amber Brown*, his favourite book. After his presentation a number of kids wanted to borrow it.

On his way back home he caught Martin standing on a ladder underneath one of the library windows. But that was not his only surprise that evening.

A message was waiting for him on the kitchen table.

Leo,
A certain Mrs Rivers rang for you. From Mosquito Lake. She passed on the number of someone called Marie: 541 466 6666.

Who is this Marie? And who is Mrs Rivers?
I hope you are well. I will be back late, but
we can talk about this tomorrow morning.
Mum

Leo's heart did a somersault and three pirouettes. He wanted to ring Marie straight away. So he called her number. The phone at the other end was ringing. After five rings someone answered. He recognized Marie's voice.

He hung up immediately. All of a sudden he had lost his courage, his nerve, his self-confidence. All of a sudden he was afraid. Very afraid. Afraid Marie might not remember who he was, afraid she might not feel like talking to him and hang up on him.

"Tomorrow... maybe. Tomorrow I'll ring her again," he promised himself.

As things turned out, he *did* ring Marie the next day, but it was not quite as he had foreseen, because that day a tragic event took place in the library of Saint-Anatole.

Chapter 11

Wake up, Miss Charlotte!

Leo found it hard to fall asleep. He kept hearing the voice of Marie at the other end of the line.

He would do anything to stop being shy! He was angry with himself for having hung up.

Still, he woke up in quite a good mood, because it was Saturday. No English or maths, no times tables or spelling.

He got dressed quickly and scoffed down a few slices of toast with Nutella and drank two big glasses of raspberry juice before setting off to the library.

When he arrived, everything seemed normal. A number of children were reading books on air mattresses or in hammocks. Pierre and Sophie were repairing old tatty books, while Julien fed the mice and his brother Theo cleaned the guinea-pig cage. Some children were exploring the loft, looking for new books to read, while others were preparing loads of snacks.

Leo guessed Miss Charlotte was on a journey in one of her books when he saw her spindly legs sticking out of the tent he had brought to the library.

"No need to wake her up: she's in no danger," said Matthieu, who was sitting next to her, reading a book.

At noon, Pierre invited Leo and some other mates to a sandwich shop. For his birthday Pierre had received a voucher for twenty hotdogs. They stuffed themselves with free hotdogs with ketchup and played some footie in the park behind the empty parking lot of the Town Hall.

When they returned to the library, Miss Charlotte was still lying stretched out in the tent with a book in her hand. The children began to worry.

"Normally she wakes up after an hour or two," Leo said.

"She was already absorbed by her book when I arrived this morning," Sophie added.

"Maybe she hasn't eaten a thing all day today, or had anything to drink," said Julien, who is always thinking about food.

Leo had a funny feeling about this. He hurried towards the tent and let out a cry. Miss Charlotte was holding *Beauty and the Beast*, the same book Leo had found it so hard to rescue her from.

He remembered Miss Charlotte's massive crush on the Beast.

"I would *love* to live by his side and never ever leave him!" she had told him in secret.

Leo realized just how serious the situation was.

"Quickly! We must wake her up. Otherwise she may never come back."

Leo took the book and started reading the story out loud, putting his heart and soul into it. He read the bit where Beauty discovers that, while she was away, the Beast had nearly starved himself to death.

The children listened intensely, moved by the immense suffering of the Beast.

But Miss Charlotte did not wake up.

At his wits' end, Leo read the same passage again. It was as if he were part of the story himself – that's how convincing and real his voice sounded.

But Miss Charlotte did not wake up.

Big tears were streaming down Lily's face.

"Do *th*omething, Leo, plea*th*e! She mu*tht* come back," she pleaded.

All eyes were on Leo. The children were afraid they would never see Miss Charlotte again.

"Marie!" Leo shouted all of a sudden. "We have to ask Marie for help."

Leo spurted to the door and ran all the way to his house, leaving his friends to wonder just *who* this mysterious Marie might be.

Chapter 12

Dear Door Handle

Marie heard the phone ring as she was going through her pockets looking for her house key. But just when she burst into the kitchen to pick up the phone, it stopped ringing.

"Aw, fudge!" she exclaimed. "I wonder who that was."

Her dad never rang her from his work, and she didn't really have any friends, because she had only just moved to this town.

Marie felt sad. She was fed up of moving house and changing towns, schools and friends. Of finding herself all alone in a class where everyone already knows each other and where everyone

is having a good time and has plenty of friends.

She stuck her hand into her pocket, feeling for Gertrude. She grabbed the pebble and caressed it softly with her fingers.

"If only you knew how much I'd give to see Miss Charlotte again. You miss her too, don't you?"

The telephone rang again.

Marie picked up immediately.

"Marie? Is that you?"

"Yes… Who is speaking?"

"It's Leo."

"Leo from the Explorers' Camp?"

"That's me!" Leo burst out, over the moon that Marie remembered him.

He would have liked to talk about all the letters he had written to her. About all the times he had thought of her. But this was not the moment.

"Look, Marie, I abso-
lutely need your help. It's
urgent."

As clearly and briefly
as he could, Leo told her
about the new librarian,
and everything that
had happened since her
arrival.

"It's her all right. I'm
sure of it," said Marie.

"But she doesn't have a pebble underneath
her hat," Leo pointed out.

"Of course not! *I* have her pebble now. She
passed it on to me," Marie replied, laughing.
"But where are you? We need to help Miss
Charlotte."

"In my hometown, Saint-Anatole."

"Saint-Anatole? Between St Cuthbert and
Shrimp-Regis?"

"Yes…"

"I live just round the corner!" Marie
exclaimed. "I'll be there right away. Wait for

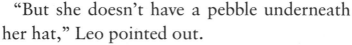

me at the library. I'll be there in under thirty minutes."

Marie put Gertrude in her pocket, took her bicycle helmet, which was lying in the hallway, dashed out of the door and jumped on her bike. Seven and a half miles! With a bit of luck she'd be there in twenty-five minutes. Marie

had been training every day for weeks, doing twenty-five miles a day to prepare herself for a big race.

"Come on, Germain! Let's see what you can do!" she said to her bike in order to encourage it.

Ever since Miss Charlotte had left, Marie had started to talk not just to Gertrude, but also to her bike, her scarf, her toothbrush, her gloves, the kitchen broom and even the door handle...

Chapter 13

It's Up to You Now, Gertrude

Leo couldn't stop looking at his watch. His heart was pounding like mad. Marie had been cycling for twenty-two minutes. A crowd of children was waiting for her at the Town Hall.

Then, suddenly, a blue bike came careering down the hill. It was Marie! The children cheered her on and Marie was filled with happiness.

No sooner had she got off her bike than Leo took her by the hand and led her to the library in the loft. Although Marie's head was swimming with emotions, she was still impressed by the place. Surely there was no other library quite like it.

"Miss Charlotte!" she cried out suddenly when she saw her old teacher stretched out on the floor.

"We've done all we could to wake her up," the other children whimpered.

"Leo *th*ays it's becau*th*e she's in love with the mon*th*ter in *Beauty and the Beatht*," Lily explained.

Marie knew that beautiful story well. She understood why Miss Charlotte had fallen head over heels in love with the Beast.

"I know what to do," said Marie.

She dug her hand into her pocket and got out a rock.

"It's up to you now, Gertrude," she whispered to the precious pebble, while the other children were wondering whether this odd girl was perhaps even stranger than their new librarian.

"Are you completely bonker*th* too?" Lily wanted to know.

Marie didn't even hear her. Her eyes were fixed on the pebble, which she placed in Miss Charlotte's hand. Then, very softly, she folded her old teacher's fingers over it.

The silence that followed was so long and profound that even the mice, the spiders, the guinea pigs and the dwarf rabbits didn't move a muscle. They were all waiting for what would happen next.

Miss Charlotte didn't move. She didn't yawn or stretch herself. But the children saw a teeny-weeny tear well up in the corner of her right eye. Gently it rolled down Miss Charlotte's wrinkled cheek. When she woke up, her eyes shone like grass after a rain shower.

"You did well to come and find me," she told the kids as she slowly got up. "I love the Beast, but he has already given his heart away."

Miss Charlotte sighed very deeply, and then she turned to Leo and Marie.

"Thanks, especially to you two," she said.

A mysterious smile played on her lips.

"And thanks to my beautiful Gertrude," she added, tickling her pebble in a funny kind of way.

Epilogue

That summer Leo covered many miles on his bike, accompanied by Marie. They also swapped lots of books and went to see Miss Charlotte every day. Sometimes even at night, in secret. The strange old lady confessed all sorts of extraordinary things, and the two friends discovered that she was even more amazing than they had imagined.

Marie wanted to return Gertrude to Miss Charlotte, but she refused.

"No. You keep her. Maybe one day you will need her."

"But what if *you* need her one day? If you were sucked up by one of your books again and ran the risk of never coming back?" Marie replied anxiously.

Miss Charlotte shook her head.

"I've learnt that characters in books live in another world. You can travel around in a book, but you have to accept that you can't stay there."

That night, Miss Charlotte behaved even more strangely than normal. When Leo and Marie left the library, she made them promise to look after Martin. The two friends wondered why.

The next day they found Martin stretched out on the floor of the library, not moving and with a book in his hands.

Leo and Marie looked for Miss Charlotte in all the nooks and crannies of the loft.

At last they found a message pinned up above her bed.

Dear friends,
Take care of yourselves and Gertrude, and of this loft, which is a treasure trove. Big hugs to all my friends.
I absolutely have to leave. A new adventure is waiting for me. But, who knows, maybe

one day we will see each other again. I really hope so.

Whatever happens, I will never forget you and will always love you.

Miss Charlotte

THE END

Chapter 1

She's Completely Bonkers!

Normally teachers walk very fast. They're always in a hurry. Their heels go click! clack! click! clack! click! in the corridor. That morning, it was different. Our new teacher seemed to take her time. We heard two or three little tap-taps. Then, nothing. As if our new teacher were dawdling in the corridor instead of hurrying up.

The class was silent. You could have heard a pea roll across the floor. We were all dying with curiosity to see what our new teacher looked like. We'd been talking about nothing else all week. No one knew what this mysterious person from another town might look like. Our old teacher was having a baby. She'd left us to look after her big round tummy.

Suddenly the door opened and a very tall and very thin lady appeared. She was wearing a strange hat. It was like a witch's hat, except that the top was round instead of long and pointy. Her dress, however, was nothing like a witch's outfit. It was an old-fashioned evening gown with bows and lace, a bit faded but still pretty.

And that was not all. Our new teacher didn't wear tiny shoes with high heels like the others. She was wearing big leather ones with thick soles. These were shoes made for hiking in forests, climbing up mountains or walking to the ends of the earth... Not for going to school at any rate.

We all opened our eyes as wide as planets, and quite a few jaws dropped too. As always, it was Alex who spoke first.

"She's not a teacher: she's a scarecrow!"

Some of us chuckled. Then, nothing. Our eyes were riveted on that weird old lady. She slowly walked to the window, the one from where you can see the little wood where

Matthieu and Julie meet to kiss. Our new teacher looked out of the window. Then she smiled. She had a lovely smile.

Normally teachers present themselves. They say: "Good morning children, I am Mrs Lagalipette." Or else: "Hello, my name is Nathalie." Their voice is soft or shrill, their tone harsh or cheerful. You get an idea who you're dealing with. But our new teacher didn't say a word.

She went to her desk, and then I realized she didn't even have a bag with books or anything. That funny old teacher had come to school empty-handed! If we forget our school bag, we have to go and see the head teacher, Mr Cracpote, and explain why. I always find that a little difficult, because if you forget something, you forget something. That's all there is to it. You can't really explain why.

Then at last our beanpole of a teacher sat down. Everyone was holding their breath. We'd finally find out if she was obsessed with maths or with spelling tests. Or if she was the kind who makes a fuss about nothing.

There are teachers who go berserk when words go any which way on the page instead of neatly staying on the lines of our exercise books. Others panic at the slightest noise. A mouse's fart would wake them up at night.

What I wanted to find out most of all was if our new teacher liked – a little, a lot or an awful lot – to put people in detention. Because with the old one, let's just say I got my fair share.

Our new teacher was now well and truly installed behind her desk, but she didn't seem to be in a hurry. She quietly smoothed out the hem of her dress and then, without even looking at us, she delicately took off her huge hat, holding it by its broad brim, and placed it on the desk.

Her grey hair was held together in a bun. She wore her hair like many old ladies do, except that she had a strange object on her head. It was the size of, say, a tangerine, a golf ball or a big marble. A few pupils got up to have a better look, and Benoît even climbed onto his desk.

It was a pebble!